WORDS ARE MAGIC!

by Zaila Avant-garde

illustrated by Felicia Whaley

Random House New York

Words are magic!

Have you heard?

Dear Parents:

Congratulations! Your child is taking the first steps on an exciting journey. The destination? Independent reading!

STEP INTO READING® will help your child get there. The program offers five steps to reading success. Each step includes fun stories and colorful art or photographs. In addition to original fiction and books with favorite characters, there are Step into Reading Non-Fiction Readers, Phonics Readers and Boxed Sets, Sticker Readers, and Comic Readers—a complete literacy program with something to interest every child.

Learning to Read, Step by Step!

Ready to Read   Preschool–Kindergarten
• big type and easy words • rhyme and rhythm • picture clues
For children who know the alphabet and are eager to begin reading.

Reading with Help   Preschool–Grade 1
• basic vocabulary • short sentences • simple stories
For children who recognize familiar words and sound out new words with help.

Reading on Your Own   Grades 1–3
• engaging characters • easy-to-follow plots • popular topics
For children who are ready to read on their own.

Reading Paragraphs   Grades 2–3
• challenging vocabulary • short paragraphs • exciting stories
For newly independent readers who read simple sentences with confidence.

Ready for Chapters   Grades 2–4
• chapters • longer paragraphs • full-color art
For children who want to take the plunge into chapter books but still like colorful pictures.

STEP INTO READING® is designed to give every child a successful reading experience. The grade levels are only guides; children will progress through the steps at their own speed, developing confidence in their reading. The F&P Text Level on the back cover serves as another tool to help you choose the right book for your child.

Remember, a lifetime love of reading starts with a single step!

To my little brothers,
who inspired this book —Z.A.

To my daughter, whose
first word was EAT —F.W.

Text copyright © 2024 by Zaila Avant-garde
Cover art and interior illustrations copyright © 2024 by Felicia Whaley

All rights reserved. Published in the United States by Random House Children's Books,
a division of Penguin Random House LLC, New York.

Step into Reading, Random House, and the Random House colophon are registered trademarks
of Penguin Random House LLC.

Visit us on the Web!
rhcbooks.com

Educators and librarians, for a variety of teaching tools, visit us at RHTeachersLibrarians.com

Library of Congress Cataloging-in-Publication Data
Names: Avant-garde, Zaila, author. | Whaley, Felicia, illustrator.
Title: Words are magic! / by Zaila Avant-garde ; illustrated by Felicia Whaley.
Description: New York : Random House Children's Books, [2024] | Series: Step into reading |
Audience: Ages 3–6 | Summary: "Scripps National Spelling Bee champion Zaila Avant-garde
teaches young readers about the joy of learning new words in this Step 1 leveled reader."
—Provided by publisher.
Identifiers: LCCN 2023004118 (print) | LCCN 2023004119 (ebook) |
ISBN 978-0-593-57167-5 (paperback) | ISBN 978-0-593-57168-2 (lib. bdg.) |
ISBN 978-0-593-57169-9 (ebook)
Subjects: LCSH: Readers (Primary) | Children's writings | LCGFT: Readers (Publications)
Classification: LCC PE1119.2 .A93 2024 (print) | LCC PE1119.2 (ebook) |
DDC 428.6/2—dc23/eng/20230217

Printed in the United States of America
10 9 8 7 6 5 4 3 2 1
First Edition

This book has been officially leveled by using the F&P Text Level Gradient™ Leveling System.

Pick a letter.

Make a word!

Bat

Hat

Cat

You can sing words!

Sing

Sing

You can shout words!

Draw them!

Paint them!

Touch them!

14

Trace them!

15

You can build words.

18

You can stack words.

You can mix words.

You can match words.

Can you read them?

Can you find them?

Can you spell them?

Can you rhyme them?

Fun to rap words!

Fun to write words!

goodnight

Cuddle up and
say goodnight words!

BANK
BOOKSTOR
burger
BUS
STOP
ROUTE
MAIN ST.
PIZZA
TAXI
TAXI
0123

Words, words, words!
Words are everywhere!

I love words!

Sing

Build

Read

Stack

Draw

Paint